THE PAINTER'S CAT

Written and illustrated by Sharon Wooding

G. P. Putnam's Sons   New York

For Jerry

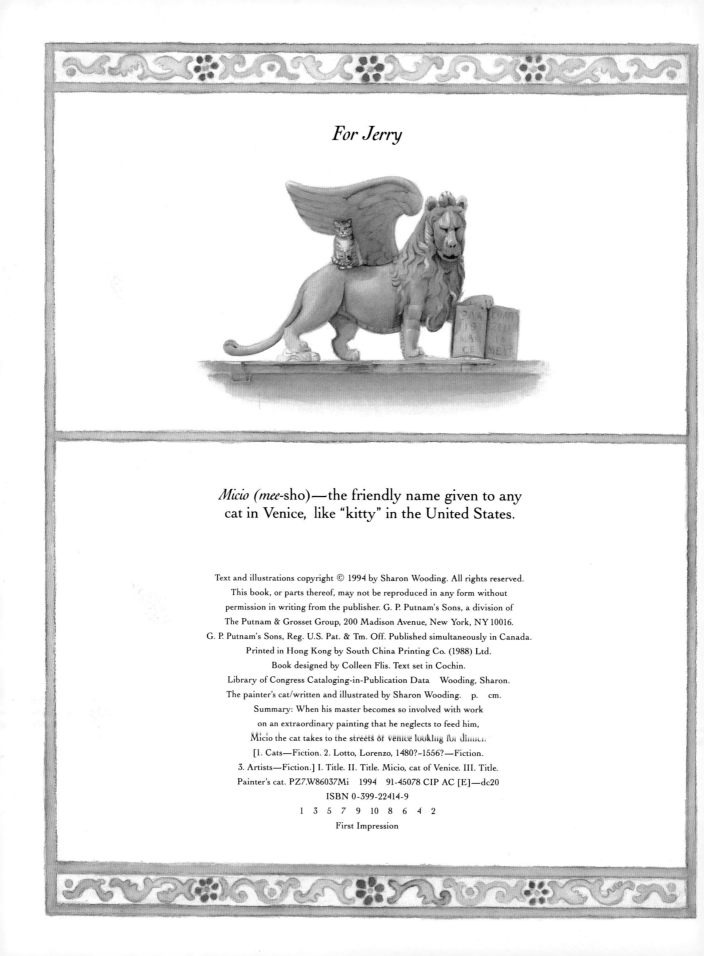

*Micio (mee-*sho)—the friendly name given to any
cat in Venice, like "kitty" in the United States.

Text and illustrations copyright © 1994 by Sharon Wooding. All rights reserved.
This book, or parts thereof, may not be reproduced in any form without
permission in writing from the publisher. G. P. Putnam's Sons, a division of
The Putnam & Grosset Group, 200 Madison Avenue, New York, NY 10016.
G. P. Putnam's Sons, Reg. U.S. Pat. & Tm. Off. Published simultaneously in Canada.
Printed in Hong Kong by South China Printing Co. (1988) Ltd.
Book designed by Colleen Flis. Text set in Cochin.
Library of Congress Cataloging-in-Publication Data   Wooding, Sharon.
The painter's cat/written and illustrated by Sharon Wooding.   p.   cm.
Summary: When his master becomes so involved with work
on an extraordinary painting that he neglects to feed him,
Micio the cat takes to the streets of Venice looking for dinner.
[1. Cats—Fiction. 2. Lotto, Lorenzo, 1480?–1556?—Fiction.
3. Artists—Fiction.] I. Title. II. Title. Micio, cat of Venice. III. Title.
Painter's cat. PZ7.W86037Mi   1994   91-45078 CIP AC [E]—dc20
ISBN 0-399-22414-9
1   3   5   7   9   10   8   6   4   2
First Impression

M icio stared sadly out the window of the monastery. Lorenzo, his master, who had taken him in from the streets a year before, didn't seem to need him anymore. Micio's stomach rumbled.

He jumped down from the ledge and rubbed himself against Lorenzo's legs. No response. He purred loudly, but Lorenzo didn't even look away from his work.

A drop of *polenta* spilled off the artist's table and Micio lunged for it. Pheh! Spoiled! Micio batted it away.

When the apprentice came to grind Lorenzo's colors for him, Micio caught his eye. The boy gave him a scratch under the chin. "There, there, little Micio," he said. And he started to pour a bowl of milk.

But then Lorenzo shouted from the other room. "Where are you, Paolo—I can't wait all day! I'm working on something important!" So the apprentice dropped what he was doing and never came back.

An hour later there was a knock at the door. Lorenzo jumped up from his sketching to answer.

Micio froze. There stood a man with a grizzled beard, a woman in a red dress, and an enormous creature with wings!

"*Buon giorno,*" Lorenzo said to the terrible strangers. "Come in and sit down while I get you some refreshment."

Refreshment? *REFRESHMENT!* This was too much! He couldn't mean to feed them first. Micio followed Lorenzo into the kitchen to see for his own eyes. It was true. And to make matters worse, the monster with wings was going to have his snack *in Micio's chair!*

Micio tried to get the creature's attention by swatting him with his paw. When that didn't work he tried just a tiny bit of claw....

"Owww!" howled the monster.

"Bad cat!" scolded Lorenzo. "Scat!" And he picked Micio up and plunked him down outside the door.

Micio was insulted.

Micio left home.

Up and down the streets of Venice he wandered until he came upon some children playing. Aha! he thought, if I amuse them with some tricks maybe they'll feed me.

It seemed to be going well, until the youngest one grabbed his tail! Whoosh! down the narrow street he sped.

Micio came to a market near a wide and splendid canal. At one stand a woman was selling loaves of rich brown bread.

He reached for one with both paws, but...

SWAT! Before you could say *"prego,"* the woman sent him sprawling.

Micio's whiskers drooped. His stomach had given up growling and settled into a steady ache. But he plodded on.

"*Buona sera*," said a friendly man, tossing Micio a fish. At last! He pounced on his morsel and licked the salty scales.

Suddenly a black clump of fur came crashing down from nowhere. Micio hissed and cried in protest, but then more cats came, yowling and yanking at the fish. Poor Micio gave up and headed back to the alleyways.

And so it went for Micio as he strayed through the city looking for food, shying from the rain. But he only grew thinner and lonelier as the days went by.

Then finally, one black night, as he sat in the doorway with raindrops rolling off his whiskers, Micio saw a familiar boot. It was Paolo, whistling as he walked. And before he knew it, Micio was following.

When they reached the monastery, Micio stopped under Lorenzo's room. Lightning lit the sill as Micio jumped up. He pushed aside the unlatched shutters and stepped around a puddle gathering inside. A fat, guttering candle lit part of the room with a weak, unsteady light. But it led Micio to Lorenzo.

The painter lay asleep at his drawing table, pictures piled about him and half covering his face, like a paper blanket.

Cautiously, Micio hopped up and padded softly over the papers. With a gentle swipe he uncovered a drawing of a cat. Wait. Not just any cat. Micio. Picture after picture he uncovered. Micio sleeping. Micio eating...and one of Micio leaping into the air, with a look of terror on his face.

Finally, Micio noticed Lorenzo's canvas, which was now turned toward the center of the room. And for the first time Micio knew what his master had been working on all these weeks: an extraordinary painting of the man with the beard, the woman in red, the creature with wings, and of Micio, himself, right in the middle of everything.

"Do you like it?" Lorenzo asked, lifting his sleepy head. "It took me a while. I am very tired." The artist took a long look at Micio.

"You have been gone too long, my friend, but it's good to have you back. I am sorry if I neglected you." Lorenzo stroked his fur.

"You're wet," he said. With a soft towel he gently dried Micio off. He lit a fire and put Micio's favorite cushion by the grate. Then he put out a tray of fresh fish and a bowl of milk, and made himself a mug of something hot.

"Here's to you, Micio," he said, raising the drink. "Here's to my favorite model."

Micio looked up from the fish long enough to blink his eyes in return. It was hard work being part of a great painting. But sometimes it was worth it.

Author's Note

This make-believe story is about a real painting called "The Annunciation." It can be seen today in a church in the town of Recanati, Italy, which is south of Venice.

The artist was a Venetian painter called Lorenzo Lotto, who lived in different parts of Italy between 1480 and 1556, and often stayed at the monastery of Santi Giovanni e Paolo when he was in Venice.

No one knows for sure where the cat in Lotto's painting came from. But it could be that Lorenzo, needing a model to draw from, did indeed adopt one of the many cats who roamed the narrow streets of Venice in the 1500s. And that cat could very well have been Micio.

Acknowledgments

For their invaluable help and encouragement, I would like to thank Arthur Levine, Kendra Marcus, Frances Lansing, Nanette Stevenson, Colleen Flis, Georgess McHargue and Caleb Bach. I am also most grateful to Bob French, The Groton Public Library, Mark Haman, The Harvard University Art Museums, Jane Langton, Amy Mullen, Kelly Purcell, Jean and Thano Schoppel, Cristiano Toraldo di Francia, and Kendra, Micio, Nellie and Tigger.